Rugrats™

VOLUME TWO

kaboom!™

COVER BY
JORGE CORONA

SERIES DESIGNER
MICHELLE ANKLEY

COLLECTION DESIGNER
JILLIAN CRAB

EDITORS
WHITNEY LEOPARD
MATTHEW LEVINE

SPECIAL THANKS TO **JOAN HILTY, LINDA LEE, JAMES SALERNO, ALEXANDRA MAURER** AND THE WONDERFUL TEAM AT **NICKELODEON**

kaboom!™ nickelodeon

RUGRATS Volume Two, October 2018. Published by KaBOOM!, a division of Boom Entertainment, Inc.

BOOM! Studios, 5670 Wilshire Boulevard, Suite 400, Los Angeles, CA 90036-5679. Printed in China. First Printing.

ISBN: 978-1-68415-256-8, eISBN: 978-1-64144-118-6

WRITTEN BY
BOX BROWN

CHAPTER FIVE ILLUSTRATED BY
LISA DuBOIS & MATTIA DI MEO

CHAPTERS SIX & SEVEN ILLUSTRATED BY
ILARIA CATALANI

"MUD PIE"

WRITTEN BY
PRANAS T. NAUJOKAITIS

ILLUSTRATED BY
ESDRAS CRISTOBAL

COLORS BY
ELEONORA BRUNI

LETTERS BY
JIM CAMPBELL

CHAPTER FIVE

TOMMY! THIS IS REALLY SOMETHING!

DID YOU KNOW THE WORLD IS RUN BY REPTILIAN ALIENS WHO POSE AS THE WORLD'S ELITE?

THAT'S RIGHT, KID. LIZARD-LIKE ALIENS. I KNEW IT ALL ALONG TOO!

THE WORLD'S ELITE ARE REALLY RUNNING THE WORLD, THAT'S WHY WE'RE NOT WALKING ON EASY STREET! IT'S BEEN SO OBVIOUS ALL ALONG!

DAD! YOU WERE SUPPOSED TO BE WATCHING TOMMY!

IT'S ONE THING TO SPOUT NONSENSE AND IT'S ANOTHER TO LET HIM TRASH THE PLACE--

NOW WAIT A SECOND! I HAD MY MIND BLOWN, THAT'S WHAT HAPPENED. TAKE A LOOK AT THIS.

ONE WORD: SHAPE-SHIFTING-EXTRA-TERRESTRIAL-HUMANOIDS.

OH PLEASE, THAT'S A SILLY CONSPIRACY THEORY, POP. THE INTERNET IS FULL OF THEM.
YOU HAVE TO USE SOME CRITICAL THINKING SKILLS ON THE WEB. THERE'S A LOT OF FAKE STUFF.

OH, YOU SHOULD USE YOUR CRITICAL THINKING SKILLS AND DO YOUR OWN RESEARCH!

TOMMY BELIEVES ME. RIGHT, TOMMY?

NEXT DAY.

WATCH OUT, BABY!

LOOKING AT CLOUDS IS SUCH A BABY THING TO DO. I BET YOU'RE THINKING THE CLOUDS LOOK LIKE STUFF, *HUH?*
YEAH, HOW DID YOU KNOW THAT?

BECAUSE I KNOW EVERYTHING DUMB BABIES KNOW. BUT I ALSO KNOW LIKE, EVERYTHING ABOUT ***EVERYTHING.*** SO THERE'S THAT.

THEN...DO YOU KNOW ABOUT THE ***S'EPTILLIANS...?****
*Editors note: s'eptillians = reptilians.

UH, S'EPSKILLIAN?
YEAH! GRANDPA WAS TALKING ABOUT IT. S'EPTILLIANS, THEY'RE ALIENS OR SOMETHING.
OH. **ALIENS.** YEAH. I KNOW ABOUT THEM. THEY LIVE IN SPACE.
SO THEY'RE REAL?
OH YEAH. THEY'RE AS REAL AS THIS UNICORN.
WOW. **NEAT.**

SPACE IS NOT JUST A GIANT SEA OF NOTHING, BABY. IT'S GOT A WHOLE BUNCH OF OTHER STUFF IN IT.
WHAT KIND OF STUFFS, ANGELICA?

OTHER PLANETS LIKE OURS. AND SOME OF THE PLANETS ARE FILLED WITH OTHER PEOPLE.

PEOPLE LIKE US...

...PEOPLE DIFFERENT FROM US...

...AND PEOPLE *REALLY* DIFFERENT FROM US.

"BUT THEY STILL ACT LIKE US."
I'M GOING TO HAVE A HUMANAR BIRTHDAY PARTY!

WHAT? HUMANAR! I LOVE HUMANAR! HE'S SO COOL!

YEAH, RIGHT. YOU WERE SCARED OF HUMANAR LAST TIME.

I'M DEFINITELY SCARED OF HUMANAR! HE'S SCARY!

YOU DUMB BABIES, HUMANAR IS BORING!

HOW COMES I'VE NEVER MET AN ALIEN BEFORE, ANGELICA?
YOU DUMB BABY. BECAUSE THEY LIVE ON *THEIR* OWN PLANET AND WE LIVE ON *OUR* OWN PLANET AND THAT'S THAT.

SO...IT'S LIKE HOW CHUCKIE LIVES IN HIS OWN HOUSE, AND I LIVE IN MINE?
FINALLY! HE GETS IT!

BUT GRANDPA SAYS THEY HAVE SPACE SHIPS.

SWOOSH

OH YEAH, THEY GOT SPACESHIPS FOR SURE, BUT THEY DON'T COME VISIT. LOOK.

THIS IS AMAZING!

GASP A S'EPTILLIAN!
STOP SAYING NONSENSE.

NONE OF THAT'S TRUE. I HEARD EVERYTHING YOU SAID AND YOU DON'T KNOW ANYTHING ABOUT ALIENS.
OH HERE SHE COMES, THE BIG KNOW-IT-ALL! WHAT DO YOU KNOW?!
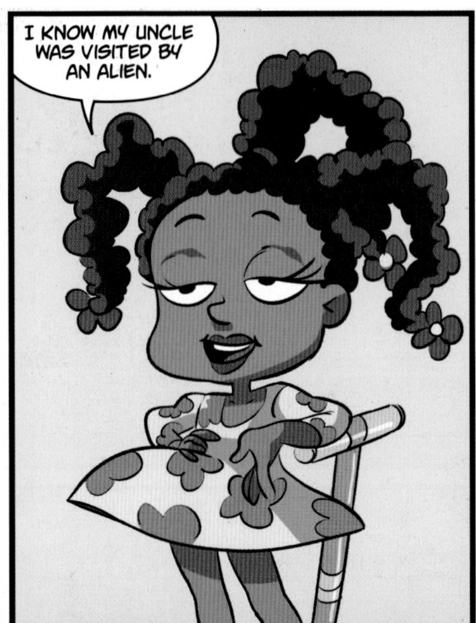
I KNOW MY UNCLE WAS VISITED BY AN ALIEN.

NO WAY!

WAY.

WHO? WHO WAS IT, SUSIE?!
WELL. I'LL TELL YA...

"WHEN MY UNCLE CHARLES WAS A KID, HE WAS SLEEPING IN HIS ROOM, WHEN SOMETHING STRANGE HAPPENED.
"HE WOKE UP TO ALL THESE LIGHTS AND SOUNDS.
"HE WENT INTO HIS BACKYARD AND THE UFO WAS OVER HIS HEAD!
"HE WASN'T SCARED AT ALL AND HE TRIED TO OFFER THE ALIENS HIS MOST PRIZED POSSESSION."
"WHAT HAPPENED NEXT, SUSIE?"
HE GOT SUCKED UP INTO THE ALIEN SPACESHIP LIKE A PIECE OF SPAGHETTI.

"THE ALIENS STUDIED HIM AND TRIED TO PUT HIM IN AN ALIEN ZOO!
"BUT HE ESCAPED AND FREED ALL THE OTHER ALIENS AND THEN GOT OUT OF THE SHIP AND GOT BACK TO HIS HOUSE. THEN THE SPACE SHIP LEFT.
"BUT IF ALIENS HAVE COME TO VISIT...THAT MEANS THEY MIGHT TRY AGAIN."
BUT I BELIEVE HIM. 'CAUSE HE'S REALLY OLD NOW. OLD PEOPLE ARE REALLY SMART AND KNOW A LOT OF STUFF.
THAT STORY IS BOGUS AND YOU KNOW IT!
WELL, SHE'S RIGHT. OLD PEOPLE ARE SMART AND KNOW A LOT OF STUFF.

THAT NIGHT.
LET'S GO, TOMMY. BEDTIME FOR BABIES! YOU BE GOOD WHILE THE GROWNUPS HAVE A LITTLE FUN.

WANNA PLAY SPACESHIP?

WHIRRRRR, BEEP BEEP, VRSHOOOOOM!

AHHHHHHH!

IT'S OKAY, TOMMY. YOU'RE OKAY. SORRY ABOUT THAT, CHAMP.

WEIRD. HE USUALLY LOVES SPACESHIP.

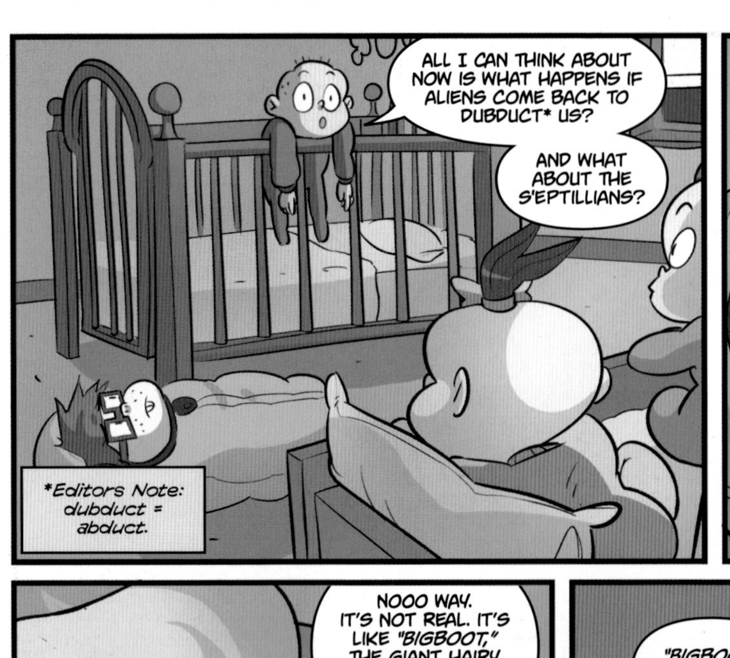

ALL I CAN THINK ABOUT NOW IS WHAT HAPPENS IF ALIENS COME BACK TO DUBDUCT* US?
AND WHAT ABOUT THE S'EPTILLIANS?
*Editors Note: dubduct = abduct.

GOSH, TOMMY. THERE'S ENOUGH SCARY STUFF HERE ALREADY!

NOOO WAY. IT'S NOT REAL. IT'S LIKE "BIGBOOT," THE GIANT HAIRY MONSTER IN THE WOODS. IT'S FAAAKE.

"BIGBOOT" IS REAL THOUGH.

IT IS NOT, PHILLIP.

IT *IS* *TOO*, LILLIAN!

IT'S *NOT*--

GUYS!

OOOoOOOOOOOo OOP OOP

WHAT'S *THAT?*

THIS IS IT! THE ALIENS ARE COMING FOR US!

I'M GETTING MY DAD! HE'S SMART HE'LL KNOW WHAT--GAH! I'M STUCK!

YEAH! THE PARENTS WILL PROTECT US FROM THE ALIENS.

NO, WE CAN'T TAKE THAT CHANCE. WHAT IF THE ALIENS GET MOM AND DAD?! WHAT IF IT'S THE S'EPTILLIANS AND THEY TAKE OVER OUR FAMILIES!

WELL I DON'T CARE. I'M USING A TIME-TESTED METHOD THAT FIXES EVERYTHING.

WAAAAAAH!

SORRY, KIDS. THE MUSIC WAS TOO LOUD, WASN'T IT? WE WERE HAVING OURSELVES A LITTLE DANCE PARTY.
STU, I TOLD YOU THE PULSATING NEON LIGHTS WERE TOO MUCH.
I GOT A LITTLE CARRIED AWAY.
THE MUSIC JUST GETS ME GOING!
MAYBE WE TURN IT DOWN A BIT, AND LOSE THE LIGHTS?
YOU KNOW WHAT...I'VE GOT AN EVEN BETTER IDEA.
OH NO...WE'RE DOING TO BE DUBDUCTED.

THERE WERE NO ALIENS! OUR PARENTS WERE JUST HAVING A FUN DANCE PARTY.
OUR PARENTS ARE STILL ACTING WEIRD, THOUGH.
MY GRANDPA SAYS SOMETIMES PEOPLE LOOK LIKE REAL PEOPLE BUT ARE ACTUALLY S'EPTILLIANS.
WOULD S'EPTILLIANS WEAR MASKS?
MAYBE.
MASKS LIKE *THAT.*
FUNKY
WOO! YOU KIDS HAVING FUN?
AAAHHH!
WHAT? DID SOMETHING SCARE YOU GUYS?

NEXT DAY.
...AND THIS ARTICLE TALKS ABOUT HOW, REPTILLIANS, THOSE LIZARD PEOPLE I WAS TELLING YOU ABOUT, HOW THEY CAN JUST TURN INTO ANYONE. LIKE YOUR MOM, FOR INSTANCE!
I REALLY THINK THIS IS TOO SCARY FOR TOMMY.

TAKE TOMMY TO THE NEW PARK. THEY JUST BUILT IT. IT'S SUPPOSED TO BE REALLY ARTISTIC AND FUN.
OH, ALRIGHT. ONLY BECAUSE I'M NOT TOTALLY CONVINCED THE GOVERNMENT ISN'T ACTUALLY SPYING ON ME THROUGH THIS LAPTOP. I NEED TO DO SOME RECONNAISSANCE WORK ANYWAY.

WHY DON'T YOU GET SOME FRESH AIR?

OK, COME ON, KID.

TOMMY, SEE THAT PERSON THERE?

THAT PERSON IS ACTUALLY A LIZARD ALIEN.

I CAN TELL HE'S ONE OF THEM. SEE, THEY ALWAYS HAVE THIS REPTILIAN LOOK IN THEIR EYES.
ALSO, ANYONE THAT WORKS FOR THE GOVERNMENT IS IMMEDIATELY SUSPECT.

THE LIZARD ALIENS PRIMARY GOAL IS TO TAKE OVER THE WORLD. SO, A LOT OF THE PEOPLE IN POWER ARE ACTUALLY REPTILIANS.

OH, HERE COMES ANOTHER ONE!

HA HA HA HA
CHUCKIE, HOW ARE WE SUPPOSED TO KNOW IF SOMEONE IS AN ALIEN LIZARD PERSON OR NOT?
OH TOMMY, REMEMBER THERE'S NO ALIENS, THE PARENTS WERE JUST HAVING A DANCE PARTY.
OH YEAH? IF THERE'S NO ALIENS THEN LET'S GO PLAY INSIDE THAT!
HEY, HEY! LET'S NOT BE HASTY HERE.
ME AND MY BIG MOUTH.
UFO!

IT'S JUST A BUNCH OF KIDS IN HERE. NO ALIENS AT ALL!
I KNEW IT. ALIENS ARE FAKE.
NOT SO FAST, CHUCKIE. WE DON'T KNOW IF ALL THESE KIDS ARE REAL KIDS. ANY OF THEM COULD BE LIZARD ALIENS!
OOOHH...
AAAHH BABIES I'M AN ALIEN FROM THE PLANET DIAPERS!
BAAAHHH!
YIPES!

BWA HAHAHA HA
YOU DUMB BABIES ARE STILL TALKING ABOUT ALIENS? GET OVER IT. THERE'S NO ALIENS.

SEE THIS? IT'S FAKE.

YOU DON'T KNOW EVERYTHING, ANGELICA!

YEAH, ANGELICA YOU DON'T KNOW HARDLY ANYTHING AT ALL.

HOW WOULD YOU KNOW ANYWAY?

MY UNCLE CHARLES TOLD ME. YOU SHOULD ASK HIM YOURSELF, HE'S HERE.

HE'S RIGHT THERE. WHY DON'T YOU GO ASK HIM ABOUT HOW HE WAS TAKEN ON THE ALIEN SPACESHIP.

WHY DON'T *YOU* ASK HIM, HE'S YOUR DUMB UNCLE.

I WANNA KNOW! I WANNA HEAR THE ALIEN STORY!
UH, I'M NOT SURE I WANNA HEAR THE STORY, MAYBE IT'S TOO SCARY FOR ME.

CHUCKIE, YOU'D BE SCARED IF YOU HEARD THE STORY OR NOT!

BOY, YOU SURE GET ME, *HUH*, PHIL?

COME ON, UNCLE CHARLES, TELL US ABOUT THE ALIENS AND THE ALIEN ZOO.

YEAH, TELL US, UNCLE CHARLES. ARE THE ALIENS REAL?

ALL I CAN THINK ABOUT NOW IS WHAT HAPPENS IF THE ALIENS COME BACK **TO DUBDUCT US.**

CHAPTER SIX

HEY, POP, WHAT'RE YOU GUYS WATCHING?
HAHA, TOMMY, LOOK HOW FAKE THIS MOONLANDING IS. YOU KNOW IT WAS ACTUALLY FILMED IN NEW JERSEY?

GASP!...NEWT JERSNEY...

LOU, CAN YOU PLEASE STOP TELLING TOMMY YOUR CONSPIRACY THEORIES?

DON'T WORRY, DEED. I'LL SET ALL THE KIDS STRAIGHT AT MINI-GOLF TODAY!

OH GREAT, GOLF. CLASSIC HANGOUT OF THE WORLD'S ELITE AKA REPTILIAN-LIZARD PEOPLE.
PYRAMIDS AND WINDMILLS IN ONE PLACE? IT'S OBVIOUS!

HISTORY'S MYSTERIES
SUPER MINI GOLF
HERE WE GO, KIDS--MINI-GOLF! ALSO KNOWN AS MINIATURE GOLF AND SOMETIMES "PUTT-PUTT." ONE OF THE FINEST GAMES WE HAVE.
THE BEST PART IS THAT WE'LL ALSO ALL LEARN SOMETHING ABOUT HISTORY. YOU KIDS ARE IN FOR A REAL TREAT!
I WONDER WHAT KINDS OF TREAT...
MAYBE IT'S MALLOWS, OR STICKY SLIME, OR SNAILS!
OR IT'S NOT A TREAT AT ALL...
THE LIZARD SHIP!

WHAT DO YOU THINK, TOMMY? THAT'S A SPHINX!
I THINK THE SPHINX STINKS. THERE'S NO TREATS HERE. WHY COULDN'T WE HAVE JUST GONE TO THE PLAYGROUND?
CAUSE WE'RE GOIN' TO HELP GRANDPA PROVE THAT LIZARD-ALIUMS* ARE REAL! EVEN THE TV SAYS SO!
*Editor's Note: aliums = aliens
TOMMY, IF THE TV SAYS SO THEN YOUR GRANDPA'S SCARY STORIES ABOUT LIZARD-ALIUMS MUST BE REAL!
SCARY DOESN'T COVER IT, CHUCKIE. IT MEANS THAT ALL WE'VE LEARNEDED HERE WILL BE COMPLETE BALONEY.
WHAT'S THAT? CHUCKY IS AFRAID OF BALONEY NOW?

SEE, THE ANCIENT EGYPTIANS BUILT THESE PYRAMIDS WAY BACK 5000 YEARS AGO. NOTICE THAT THERE ARE NO ALIENS OR LIZARD PEOPLE AROUND.

SEE TOMMY, MAYBE YOUR DAD IS RIGHT. NO LIZARDS.

I DON'T KNOW, CHUCKIE, HOW DID THEY BUILD THOSE PEER-A-MITS 5000 YEARS AGO? THEY DIDN T EVEN HAVE BIG TRUCKS BACK THEN.

YEAH, HOW DID THEY BUILD THAT WITHOUT BIG TRUCKS?

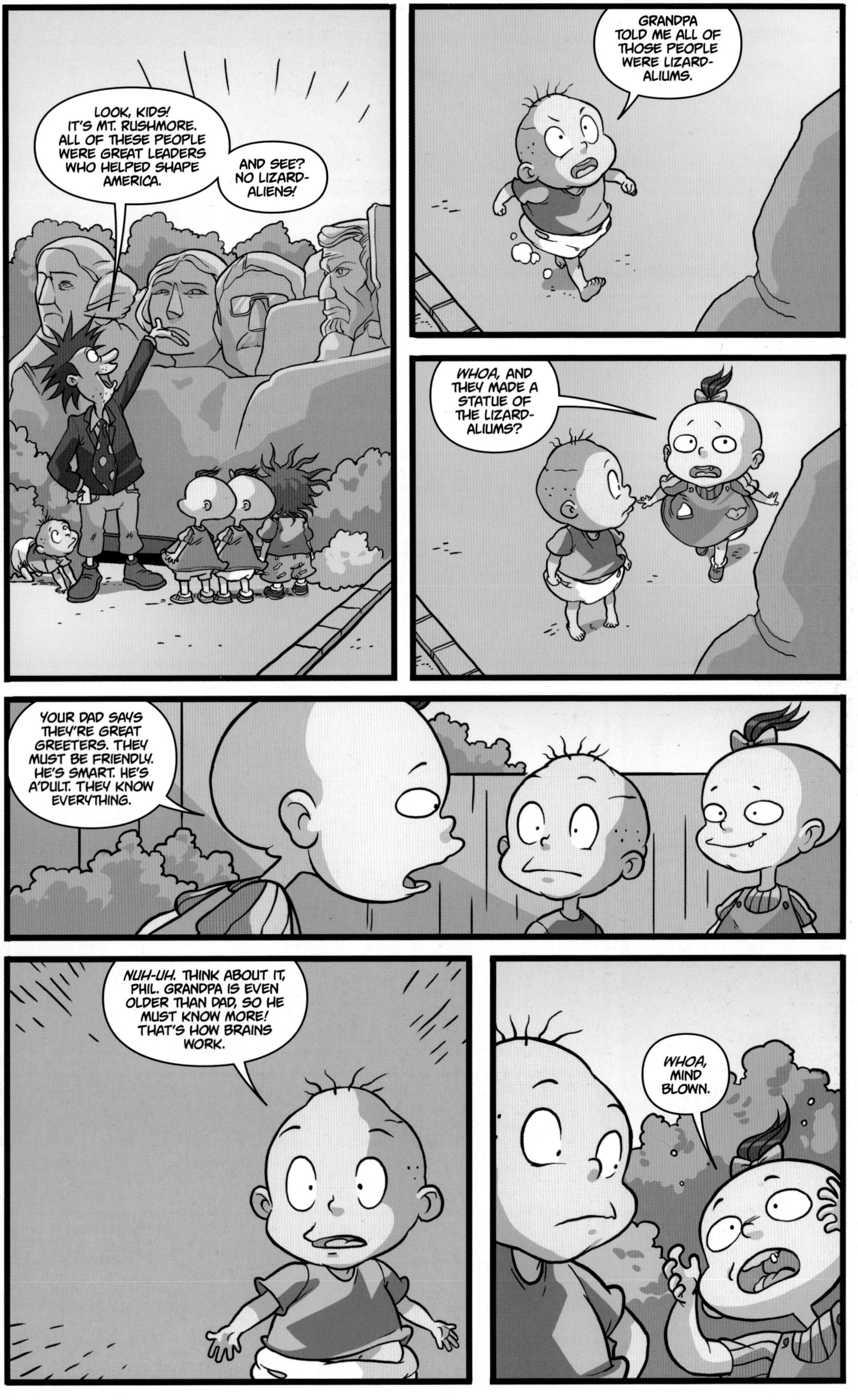

LOOK, KIDS! IT'S MT. RUSHMORE. ALL OF THESE PEOPLE WERE GREAT LEADERS WHO HELPED SHAPE AMERICA.

AND SEE? NO LIZARD-ALIENS!

GRANDPA TOLD ME ALL OF THOSE PEOPLE WERE LIZARD-ALIUMS.

WHOA, AND THEY MADE A STATUE OF THE LIZARD-ALIUMS?

YOUR DAD SAYS THEY'RE GREAT GREETERS. THEY MUST BE FRIENDLY. HE'S SMART. HE'S A'DULT. THEY KNOW EVERYTHING.

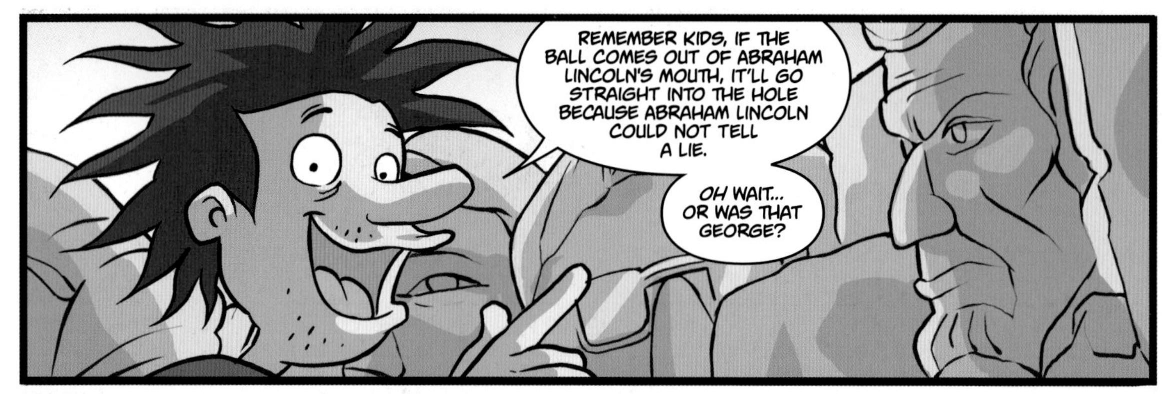
REMEMBER KIDS, IF THE BALL COMES OUT OF ABRAHAM LINCOLN'S MOUTH, IT'LL GO STRAIGHT INTO THE HOLE BECAUSE ABRAHAM LINCOLN COULD NOT TELL A LIE.
OH WAIT... OR WAS THAT GEORGE?

TOMMY, THERE'S NO WAY ALL THOSE GUYS ARE ALIUMS. IT'S JUST FOUR WISE OLD PEOPLE.

I DON'T KNOW. GRANDPA SAID THAT LIZARDS COULD BE ANYONE AND I DON'T KNOW NO HUMANS WHO SHOOT BALLS FROM THEIR MOUTHS.

I'LL PROVE IT BY MAKING HIM SPIT UP THE BALL.
I'LL TAKE THAT ACTION.

STUMP!

I SPIT UP ALL THE TIME.

SEE, KIDS, THIS WAS ONE OF THE ULTIMATE ACHIEVEMENTS OF HUMANKIND. FLYING UP TO THE MOON AND WALKING ON IT.

I KNOW YOUR GRANDPA LIKES TO SAY THIS DIDN'T HAPPEN BUT IT DID! I READ ABOUT IT IN MY HISTORY BOOKS. AND YOUR GRANDPA EVEN WATCHED IT ON TV!

SEE TOMMY, AND THE TV ALWAYS TELLS THE TRUTH.

BUT GRANDPA SAID HE SAWED IT WITH HIS OWN EYES!
HE COULDN'T HAVE SAWED IT, TOMMY!
NO, YOU CAN JUST SEE THE MOON. HE COULD HAVE JUST LOOKED UP THERE AND SEEN IT.
HMMM... YEAH YOU CAN SEE THE MOON...

MAYBE... THERE IS NO WAY TO PROVE ANYTHING.

WATCH THIS. I'M GONNA BANK IT OFF THE ASTRONAUT'S FOOT, THROUGH THE MOON LANDER'S LEGS, OFF THE AMERICAN FLAG, STRAIGHT INTO THE HOLE.

CHUCKIE, WHAT IF WE CAN'T PROVENED ANYTHING? IS IT ALL REAL?

WITH LOGIC LIKE THAT, ALIUMS MUST BE REAL!

HEY KIDS, MAYBE WHEN YOU GET A LITTLE OLDER WE'LL CHECK OUT THE HISTORY THEMED GO-KART TRACK!

I WONDER HOW MUCH YOU CAN LEARN DRIVING SO FAST AROUND THE TRACK...WOW, THEY CAN REALLY DO ANYTHING NOWADAYS.

WELL, I'M NOT EVER DRIVING ONE OF THOSE CARS. IT'S TOO FAST AND HISTORY IS TOO SCARY.

I DON'T THINK I LEARNDED ANYTHING.
YEAH, ME NEITHER.

NO, WAIT, I LEARNDED THAT IF YOU HIT THE BALL INTO THE LOG CABIN, PRESIDENT LINCOLN WILL THROW IT BACK.

YEAH, HE'S SO MEAN.

SEE TOMMY, WHAT HAPPENED WAS THIS FAMOUS FILM MAKER MADE THE MOONLANDING MOVIE. THAT'S WHY IT LOOKED SO REAL.
APOLLO

SEE, YOU CAN TELL RIGHT THERE. SEE THAT LITTLE SPEC ON THE ASTRONAUT'S HELMET? THAT'S THE MOVIE LIGHTING. EVERYONE BOUGHT IT!
TAP
TAP

LOU, WHAT ARE YOU DOING WITH TOMMY?

THAT'S IT! WE'RE GOING TO THE MUSEUM TO LEARN ABOUT *REAL HISTORY* WITHOUT GOLFING!

GREAT! I LOVE THE THEATER!

COME ON, LOU, LET'S GO!

OF COURSE, HOW COULD I FORGET!

ONE SECOND, DEEDEE!
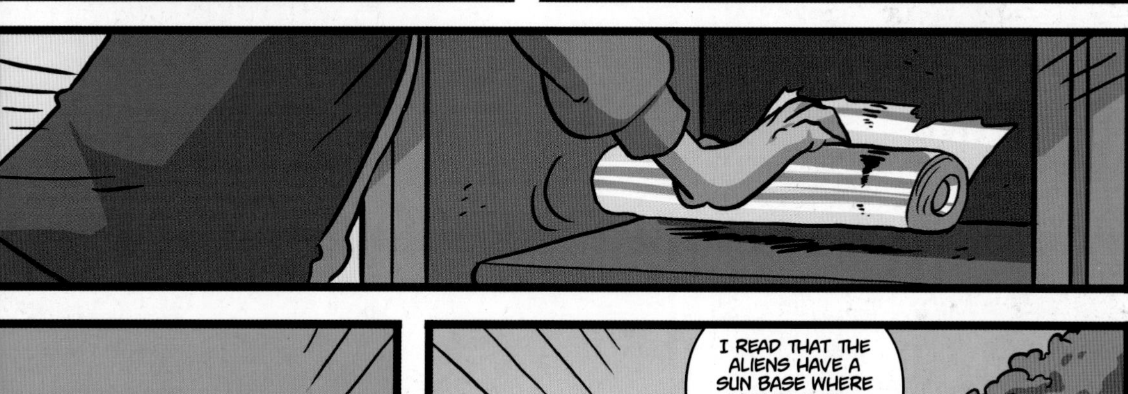

I READ THAT THE ALIENS HAVE A SUN BASE WHERE THEY CAN STEAL OUR MEMORIES THROUGH OUR EYES!

YOU KIDS ARE GOING TO HAVE SO MUCH FUN TODAY LEARNING ABOUT THE REAL TRUE NATURAL HISTORY OF THE EARTH!

PFFT...

NONE OF THAT, POP!

THIS BUSEUM* IS REALLY OLD AND HOLDS A LOT OF FACTS. IT HAS TO HAVE THE TRUTH.
*Editor's Note: buseum = museum

IF THERE ARE ALIUMS IN THE BUSEUM THEN NOWHERE IS SAFE.

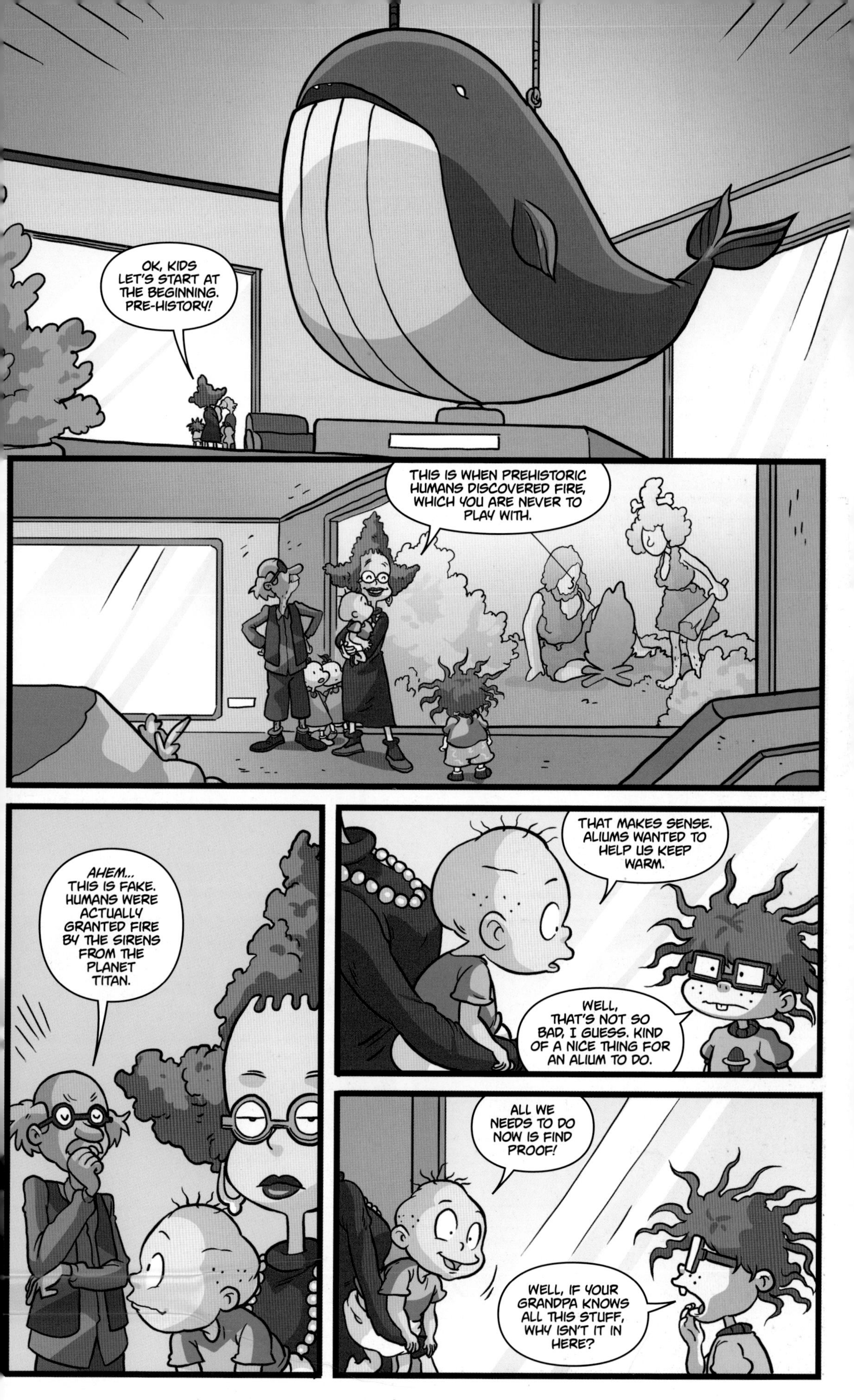

OK, KIDS LET'S START AT THE BEGINNING. PRE-HISTORY!

THIS IS WHEN PREHISTORIC HUMANS DISCOVERED FIRE, WHICH YOU ARE NEVER TO PLAY WITH.

WHY WOULD THE BUSEUM BE LYING TO US?

YEAH, IT'S A BIG BUILDING WITH LOTS OF STUFF IN IT, WHY WOULD IT LIE?
A BUILDING WOULDN'T DO THAT.

MAYBE THE BUSEUM DOESN'T KNOW WHAT GRANDPA KNOWS.

WE JUST HAVEN'T SEEN ANYTHING THAT LOOKS LIKE AN ALIUM YET. JUST REGULAR AMINALS.

WHAT ABOUT THAT, TOMMY?
YEAH, HOW DO YOU EXPLAIN THAT?

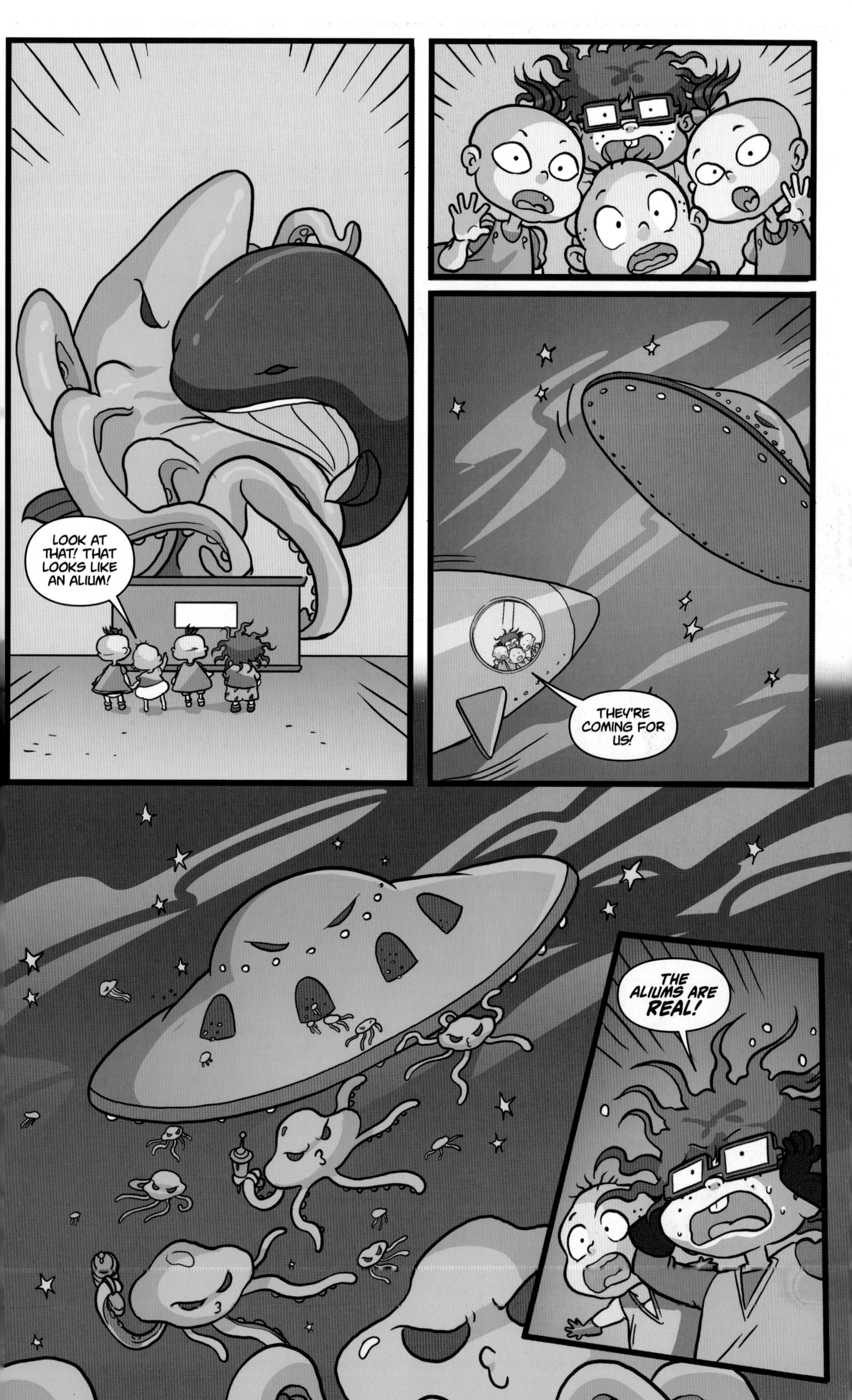
LOOK AT THAT! THAT LOOKS LIKE AN ALIUM!
THEY'RE COMING FOR US!
THE ALIUMS ARE REAL!

TAKE EVASIVE ACTION!
ACK!
THE ALIUMS ARE TRYING TO TALK TO US THROUGH THE SHIP!
COMM. SARGEANT LIL, PATCH THEM THROUGH!
PI!
HELLO WE ARE HERE.

HELLO. I AM CAPTAIN TOMMY AND I AM READY TO TALK AS LONG AS YOU DON'T WANT TO CONTROL OUR BRAINS.

OH NO, WE HAVE COME TO PURELY EXCHANGE INFORMATION.

WHAT KIND OF INFORMATION?!

WE WISH TO EXCHANGE RECIPES. WE HAVE HEARD GOOD THINGS ABOUT CHOCOLATE CHIP COOKIES.
?

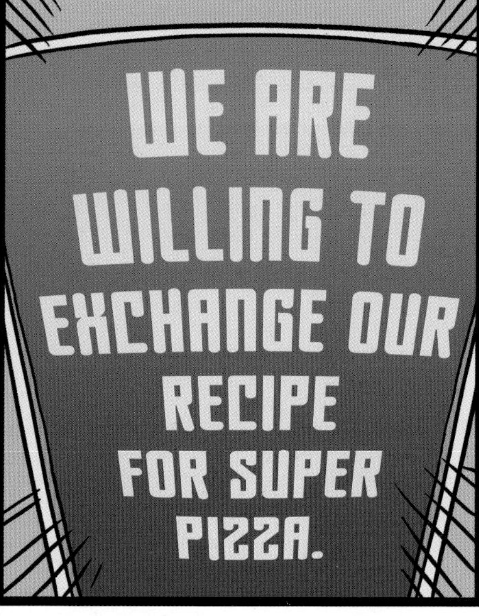
WE ARE WILLING TO EXCHANGE OUR RECIPE FOR SUPER PIZZA.

SUPER PIZZA?!?
KIDS, ARE YOU PAYING ATTENTION?

SEE, KIDS, THESE DINOSAURS LIVED ON THE EARTH MILLIONS OF YEARS BEFORE HUMANS.

THEN ONE DAY IT WAS STRUCK BY AN ASTEROID AND ALL WE HAVE LEFT ARE THESE BONES.

PFFT... ASTEROID? THERE WAS A GIANT LIZARD ALIEN WAR. THAT'S WHAT HAPPENED TO THE DINOSAURS.

SEE, TOMMY. REPTILLIAN ALIENS. GIANT LIZARDS. LOOK AT THOSE TEETH.

LOU, WATCH THE KIDS. I'M GOING TO GET EVERYONE ICE CREAM.

LOOK, TOMMY, THERE'S THAT REPTAR GUY. MAYBE HE'S ONE OF THE LIZARD ALIENS THAT CONTROL THE WORLD. THINK ABOUT IT. ASK QUESTIONS.

WOW, CHUCKIE, EVERYONE, THINK ABOUT IT. REPTAR COULD BE ONE OF THE LIZARD-ALIUMS THAT CONTROL THE WORLD!

I KNEW IT!
NO, YOU DIDN'T.

I DON'T THINK SO. REPTAR ISN'T LIKE THAT.

YOU WANT A BALLOON, SPROUT?

HE SURE SEEMS TO HAVE A LOT HE WANTS TO SAY TO YOU.

UH, HAVE A BALLOON!

AH--YOU
GIVE FIRE
TO PEOPLES?

HOW ABOUT TWO BALLOONS?

YEAH, I WOULDN'T TAKE BALLOONS FROM A LIZARD LIKE THAT, EITHER.

HEY,
WHERE
DID THEY
GO?!

HEY, KIDS! REPTAR JUST LOVES TO HAND OUT BALLOONS. LOOK, THEY'VE GOT PICTURES OF ME ON THEM. LOOK...

?
NO!

NOT AGAIN!

I'M NOT TAKING YOU OUT OF MY PAYCHECK AGAIN!

ACK!
AH!

SORRY ABOUT THE ICE CREAM, KIDS. I DON'T KNOW WHAT GOT INTO REPTAR.

I DO!

I'M NOT SURE IF THIS TRIP PROVENED ANYTHING.

IT PROVENED THAT REPTAR LIKES ICE CREAM.
AND BALLOONS!

DON'T WORRY, I THINK I HAVE A PLAN TO PROVENED THIS ONCE AND FOR ALL.

I THINK ALL THIS PROVENING IS MAKING ME CAR SICK!

HELLO, I’M CAPTAIN TOMMY
AND I’M READY TO TALK AS LONG AS YOU DON’T WANT TO CONTROL OUR BRAINS.

CHAPTER SEVEN

THIS IS WHERE THE BOUNCE HOUSE GOES, MOM!
THIS IS WHERE I'LL DO A DUET WITH MYSELF.
HERE IS WHERE WE'LL DO THE SACK RACE. I OBVIOUSLY *HAVE* TO WIN THOUGH. CUT A HOLE IN MINE!

THE NEXT DAY...
CHUCKIE, I WAS THINKING THE OTHER DAY. YOU KNOW HOW ANGELICA KIND OF CONTROLS EVERYTHING?
KIND OF?

I GUESS YOU'RE RIGHT.
YEAH, SHE ALWAYS GETS WHAT SHE WANTS.
GOSH, THIS LEVEL IS HARD.

SHE WAS TELLING HER MOMMY TO DO ALL THIS STUFF SHE WANTS FOR HER BIRTHDAY PARTY AND HER MOMMY WAS JUST... DOING IT ALL.
WHAT A NICE MOMMY ANGELICA HAS.

AREN'T YOU WONDERING WHAT I'M WONDERING?

IF WE'LL BE INVITED TO ANGELICA'S BIRTHDAY PARTY?

YOU'RE NOT USING YOUR NOODLES, CHUCKIE. GRANDPA SAYS THE PEOPLE THAT CONTROL EVERYTHING ARE LIZARD-ALIUMS,* RIGHT?
*Editor's Note: aliums = aliens

OH NO, TOMMY, NOT THIS STUFFS AGAIN.

BUT THINK ABOUT IT. IF ANGELICA CONTROLS EVERYTHING... MAYBE SHE'S A LIZARD-ALIUM TOO. SHE COULD BE HOW WE PROVE MY GRANDPA IS RIGHT!

THAT'S NOT A BAD--LOOK OUT!
RAAAR!

HAR HAR HAR!

FINAL BOSS

GAHH!
I TOLD YA THIS LEVEL WAS HARD!

WE NEED TO THROW ACORNS AT HIM TO WIN!

I REALLY DON'T SEE HOW THESE ACORNS ARE GONNA HURT THIS GIANT--

THROW THE ACORNS!
THROW THE ACORNS!

TAKE THAT!
YOU WIN!

DO YOU REALLY THINK THAT ANGELICA IS AN ALIUM?
WHY DON'T YOU ASK HER YOURSELF. HERE SHE COMES.
AHHHH!
GET UP YOU DUMB BABIES. I DON'T WANT TO HAVE A DEAD SPOT ON THE GRASS OVER HERE FOR MY PARTY.
BIRTHDAY
YOU HEAR THAT, BABY?
GULP.
OFF MY LAWN!
BIRTHDAY GIRL

LATER.
HEY, TOMMY?
YEAH, CHUCKIE?
DO YOU REMEMBER WHY WE AGREED TO PICK UP ANGELICA'S TOYS AGAIN?

WELL, WE HAD TO CLEAN UP ANYWAYS, RIGHT?
RIGHT. OF COURSE. CLEANING UP IS JUST WHAT YOU SHOULD DO WITH YOUR TOYS. SHE'S NOT THE BOSS OF US.
RIGHT, CHUCKIE. AND SHE DOESN'T HAVE LIZARD-ALIUM SIDEKICK* POWERS.
*Editor's note: sidekick = psychic.

YOU BABIES DONE CLEANING UP MY TOYS YET?
SORRY, ANGELICA!
FINISHING NOW, ANGELICA!

AND WHERE'S MY AFTERNOON CHEESE SANDWICH?!
COMING RIGHT UP, DEAR!

WE'VE GREATLY UNDERPESTIMATED* HER POWERS.
*Editor's note: underpestimated = underestimated

HOW WOULD AN ACORN DEFEAT A LIZARD ANYWAY?

SO NOW YOU THINK ANGELICA IS A LIZARD-ALIUM WHO HAS SUPER SIDEKICK POWERS AND CAN MAKE ANYONE DO WHATEVER SHE WANTS?

YUP.
BUT HOW?

YEAH, WHERE DO HER POWERS COME FROM?

I DON'T KNOW YOU GUYS. BUT I REALLY NEED THIS BOUNCE RIGHT NOW TO HELP ME SORT THINGS OUT.

I GOT IT!

SHE'S CONTROLLING EVERYONE WITH *CYNTHIA!*

NO WAY, TOMMY. THERE'S A MILLION CYNTHIA DOLLS.
YEAH, EVEN I HAVE ONE. WELL, PHIL PLAYS WITH IT.

DO NOT, LILIAN.
DO TOO, PHILIP.

EXCELLENT WORK, MOTHER AND FATHER!

HER DOLL *IS* SPECIAL. WE JUST HAVE TO FIGURE OUT HOW.

OH CYNTHIA YOU'RE A MESS. THAT'S THE LAST TIME I LET YOU TALK ME INTO DIGGING FOR WORMS.

SOMETIMES I FORGET THAT YOU'RE THE TOY AND I'M THE KID AND NOT THE OTHER WAY AROUND.
WHAT IN THE--

OOOOO, YOU DUMB BABIES!

SNATCH

WITH THE POWER OF CYNTHIA, I ORDER YOU TO NOT MOVE, ANGELICA!

YOU DUMB BABIES! HOW CAN I MOVE WITH THIS STUPID TUBE AROUND ME! AND PUT CYNTHIA DOWN!

ANGELICA, I COMMAND YOU TO LEAVE EVERYONE ALONE AND LET US MAKE SURE CYNTHIA ISN'T ALIUM TECHNOLOGY.

IS SHE TRYING TO USE HER SIDEKICK POWERS RIGHT NOW...?

HAHAHA! OH BABIES, OH MY GOSH YOU'RE SO DUMB. I FORGOT WHAT IT WAS LIKE TO BE THIS DUMB. FINE. WHATEVER. I'LL LET YOU HAVE CYNTHIA FOR ONE WHOLE HOUR IF YOU TAKE THIS SILLY POOL TOY OFF OF ME.
AND YOU BETTER NOT ACT LIKE DUMB BABIES AT MY BIRTHDAY PARTY TOMORROW!

SO WE ARE INVITED.

I HAD SOME MINOR SUCCESS WITH SPIKE, KIND OF...
...ANYBODY ELSE?

I COMMANDED THE GRASS NOT TO GROW, THAT WORKED.

HAPPY BIRTHDAY ANGELI

I GUESS ANGELICA DOESN'T GET HER POWER FROM CYNTHIA.

THAT'S GOOD TOO BECAUSE SHE'LL PROBABLY GET A LOT OF CYNTHIA TOYS TODAY. I THINK I GOT HER ONE.

HOWS ARE WE A'SPOSED TO KNOW IF SHE'S THE LIZARD-ALIUM QUEEN OR NOT NOW?

OR IF THE LIZARD-ALIUMS ARE EVEN REAL? MAYBE WE NEED TO GIVE UP, TOMMY.

I'M NOT READY TO GIVE UP, PHIL.
A BABY'S GOTTA DO, WHAT A BABY'S GOTTA DO.

TODAY, WE'RE GOING TO PROVE TO THE WHOLE WORLD THAT WE'RE ***NOT*** DUMB BABIES, THAT MY GRANDPA IS ***NOT*** A CRABPOT, AND THAT LIZARD-ALIUMS EXIST. AND WE START WITH ANGELICA.

S-STOP!

...

USED...SIDEKICK POWERS...TO MAKE...BOY... QUIT.

WELL, SHE DEFINITELY WON THE GAME BUT SHE CHEATED!
LIZARD-ALIUMS DEFINITELY CHEAT.

MOVE!

GASP!

Pi

SHE CAN CONTROL PIÑATAS? THIS MIGHT BE WHAT WILL GET PEOPLE'S ATTENTION.
IF SHE CAN CONTROL THE PIÑATA THAT MEANS...SHE CAN CONTROL THE CANDY SUPPLY!

OK, I'VE HEARD EVERYONE'S STORIES AND I THINK WE CAN NOW CONFIRM...ANGELICA IS A LIZARD-ALIUM WHO WILL EVENTUALLY GROW UP TO CONTROL THE WORLD.

SHE DEFINITELY SEEMS TO BE CONTROLLING ALL THE PEOPLE HERE AT THE PARTY.

SO WHAT DO WE DO NOW, TOMMY?
YEAH, IF ANGELICA WILL CONTROL THE WORLD THAT MEANS... EVERYONE!

IF WE CAN GET A PICTURE, MAYBE GRANDPA CAN SHOW IT TO ONE OF THE PEOPLE ON THE TV.

GREAT IDEA, TOMMY!
CAKE!

I BET THAT REPTAR HEAD WOULD BE THE BEST PIECE.
YEAH, I WANT HIS EYEBALLS!
MMM. EYEBALLS.

ANGELICA IS PROBABLY GOING TO USE HER SIDEKICK POWERS TO GET ALL OF THE GOOD PIECES. BY THE TIME IT GETS TO US IT'LL JUST BE FEET.
I'M NOT EATING REPTAR FEET AND NONE OF YOU ARE EITHER. LOOK! HERE SHE COMES!

SINCE IT'S MY BIRTHDAY I GET TO CUT THE CAKE AND I GET THE FIRST PIECE. YOU ALL CAN HAVE WHATEVER IS LEFT! HAHAHAHA.
NOW, GET IN LINE!
GET THE CAMERA READY, TOMMY!

OH NO! SHE'S GOING TO USE HER POWERS AND WE CAN'T SEE ANYTHING!
COME ON, I GOTS AN IDEA.

OOF! WE JUST GOTTA GET AROUND ALL THE BIG PEOPLES FIRST.

JEEZ. THIS KID REALLY REVELS IN POWER. YOU KNOW, SHE COULD BE ONE OF THE SECRET ALIEN RULERS OF THE WORLD.

THERE ARE TOO MANY ADULTS! WE NEED TO CLEAR A PATH.
CHUCKIE... YOU KNOW WHAT TO DO.
YOU GOT IT.

WAAAAAH!

OH NO, CHUCKIE, WHAT'S THE MATTER? DON'T WORRY. YOU'LL GET A PIECE OF CAKE... EVENTUALLY.

KH
KH
KH
KH
NO!

WE HAVE TO GET TO HIGHER GROUND!

HELP ME UP!

SHE'S... BEING NICE?

WUH-OH!

I'M NOT SURE IF ANGELICA IS A LIZARD-ALIUM ANYMORE, BUT EVEN IF LIZARD-ALIUMS DO EXIST?
MAYBE WE JUST LET THE BIG KIDS FIGURE IT OUT.
THE EN

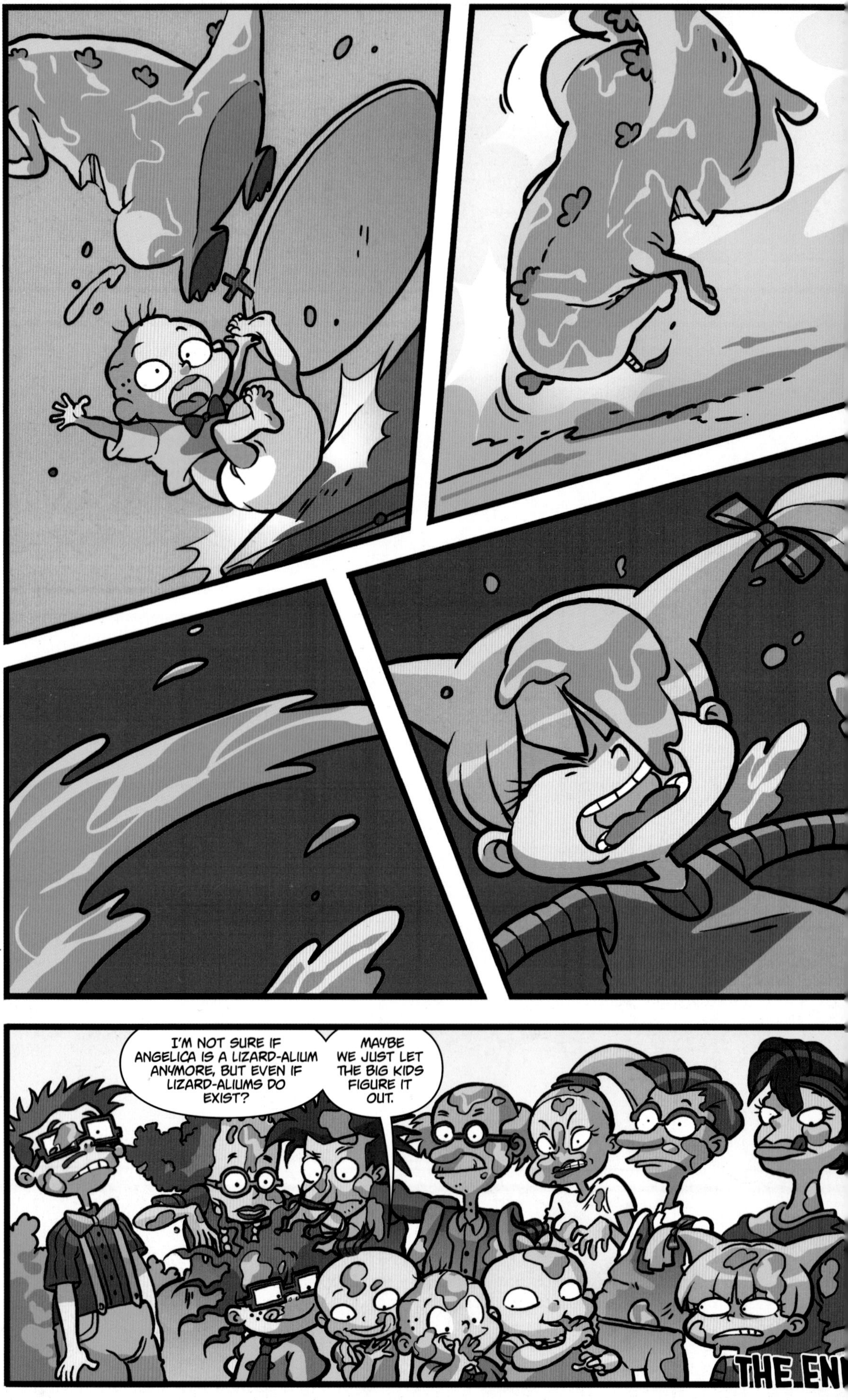

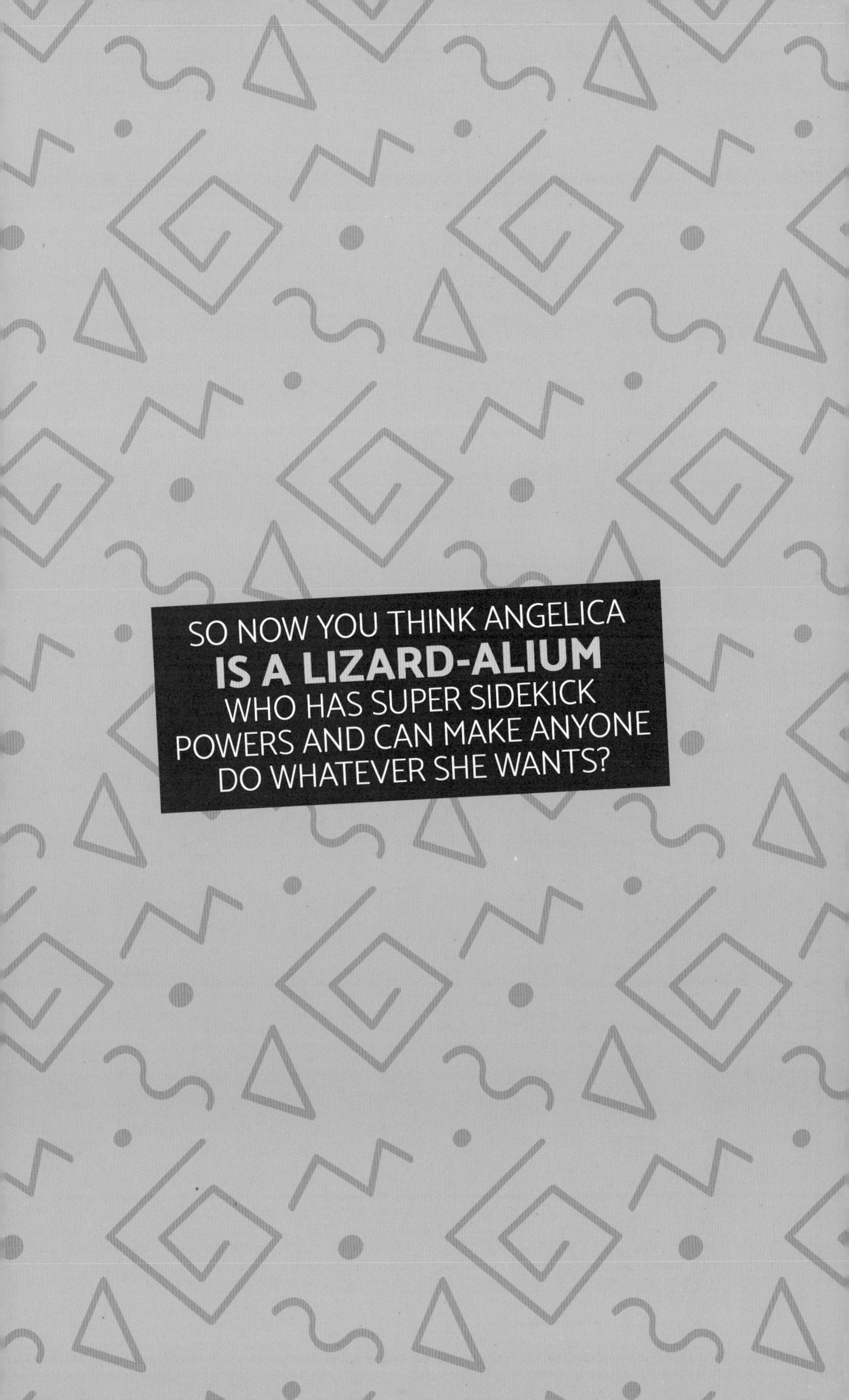
SO NOW YOU THINK ANGELICA
IS A LIZARD-ALIUM
WHO HAS SUPER SIDEKICK
POWERS AND CAN MAKE ANYONE
DO WHATEVER SHE WANTS?

MUD PIE

"OH WOW, IT SURE DID RAIN HARD LAST NIGHT!"

C'MON, CHUCKIE! THE MUD IS OH SO FINE!

CH'YEAH! THERE'S **NOTHING** LIKE A FRESH PATCH OF MUD!

IT'S ***EXTRA*** GOOPY!

AW GEEZ...

I DUNNO, GUYS! I JUST GOT THESE BRAND NEW SNEAKIES AND I DON'T WANT TO GET THEM MESSY!

BUT BEING MESSY IS THE BEST!
HA HA, YEAH!

IT'S NOT FAAAAAAAIR!
UH OH...

NOW LISTEN HERE, YOUNG LADY...
NO, I DON'T WANNA! IT'S NOT FAIR! YOU'RE NOT FAIR! THE WHOLE SYSTEM IS NOT FAIR!

ANGELICA, I AM NOT BUYING YOU AN EXPENSIVE VIDEO GAME AND THAT IS FINAL!
BUT I WANT IT!

IF YOU WANT IT SO BAD YOU CAN SAVE UP YOUR ALLOWANCE FROM DOING EXTRA CHORES.
BUT THAT WILL TAKE FOREVEEEEEERRRRRR WAAAAAH!

BRRRING
BRRRING
OH, IT'S THE OFFICE! YOU KIDS ALL PLAY NICE WHILE I TAKE THIS, I'LL BE RIGHT INSIDE.

WHAT'S WRONG, ANGELICA?
ALL I WANT IS THE NEW CYNTHIA VIDEO GAME BUT MY DAD WON'T BUY IT FOR ME!

AW, I'M SORRY, ANGELICA. BUT MAYBE YOUR DAD IS RIGHT AND IF YOU JUST DID SOME EXTRA CHORES...
WHAT?! ARE YOU KIDDING--

ANGELICA, WE MADE YOU SOMETHING!
YEAH, THIS WILL CHEER YOU UP!
HUH?

A MUD PIE!
ACK! GET THAT GROSS THING AWAY FROM ME, YOU DUMB BABIES!
WHY DID YOU THINK A CHUNK OF GROSS MUD WOULD MAKE ME FEEL BETTER?!
TOLD YA WE SHOULDA PUT IN EXTRA WORMS!
DON'T BE SILLY. WE ALL KNOW THE SECRET IS IN THE GRASS CLIPPINGS!
NUH UH, IT'S ALL ABOUT THE WORMS!
IT'S IN THE GRASS!
WORMS!
GRASS!
UH, HELLO. I DON'T MEAN TO INTERRUPT YOUR PLAYTIME, BUT...IS THAT A MUD PIE?
IT SURE IS!
FINEST AND GROSSIEST MUD PIE IN ALL THE LAND!

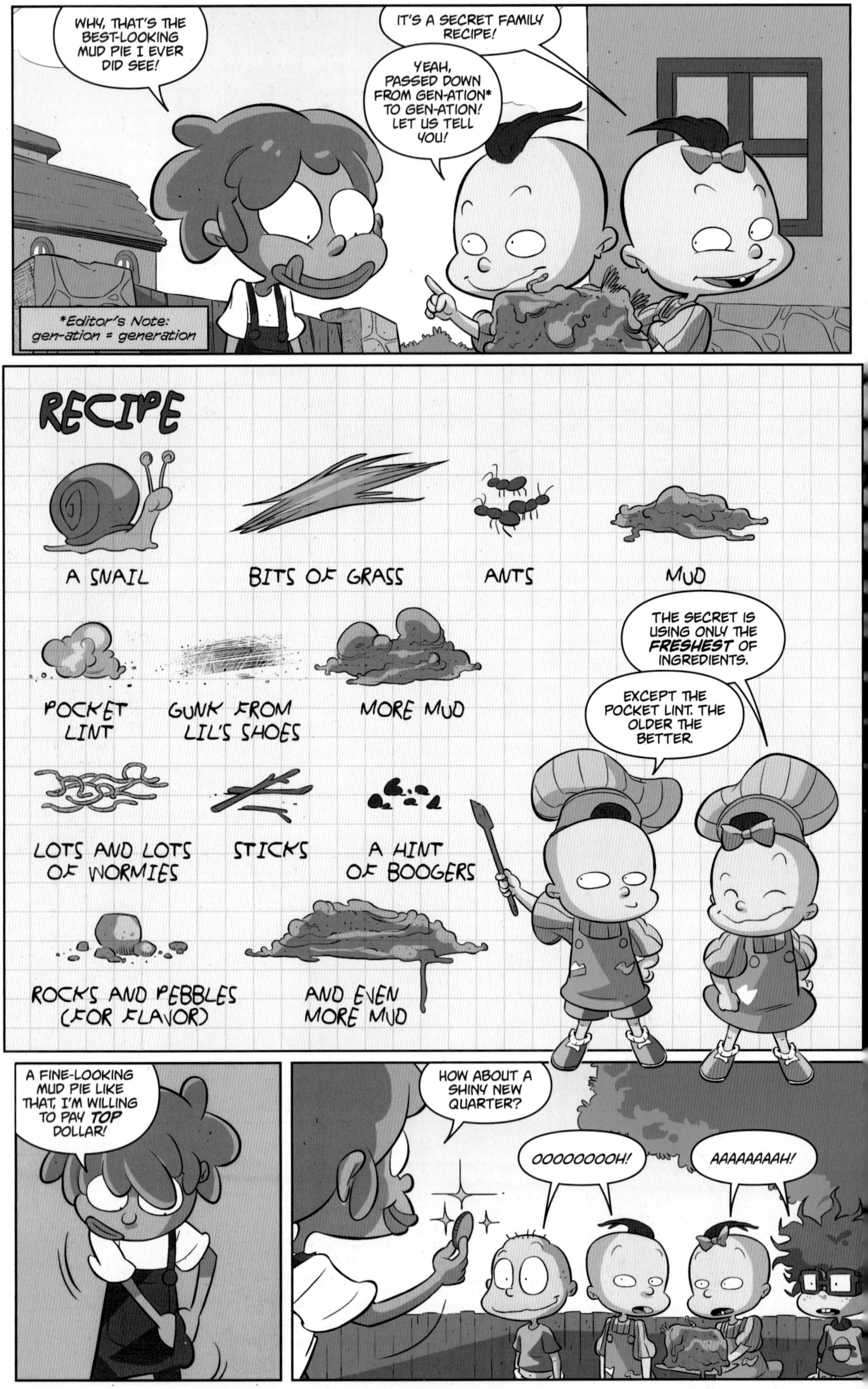

RECIPE

A SNAIL

BITS OF GRASS

ANTS

MUD

THE SECRET IS USING ONLY THE ***FRESHEST*** OF INGREDIENTS.

POCKET LINT

GUNK FROM LIL'S SHOES

MORE MUD

EXCEPT THE POCKET LINT. THE OLDER THE BETTER.

LOTS AND LOTS OF WORMIES

STICKS

A HINT OF BOOGERS

ROCKS AND PEBBLES (FOR FLAVOR)

AND EVEN MORE MUD

A FINE-LOOKING MUD PIE LIKE THAT, I'M WILLING TO PAY ***TOP*** DOLLAR!

HOW ABOUT A SHINY NEW QUARTER?

OOOOOOOOH!

AAAAAAAAH!

GIMME GIMME GIMME!

DEAL!

MMMM, THANKS!

HEH HEH HEH...ALL MINE!
AW, ANGELICA, WE WOULD'VE JUST GIVEN HIM THAT MUD PIE.
OH, REALLY? WELL...
OH GEEZ, I DON'T LIKE THAT LOOK!

YOU BABIES LIKE MAKING MUD PIES. AND I LIKE MAKING MONEY!
SO HOW ABOUT WE GO INTO BUSINESS TOGETHER, HUH? YOU WORRY ABOUT MAKING PIES AND I'LL WORRY ABOUT ALL THAT BORING GROWN UP BID-NESS STUFF! EVERYBODY WINS!

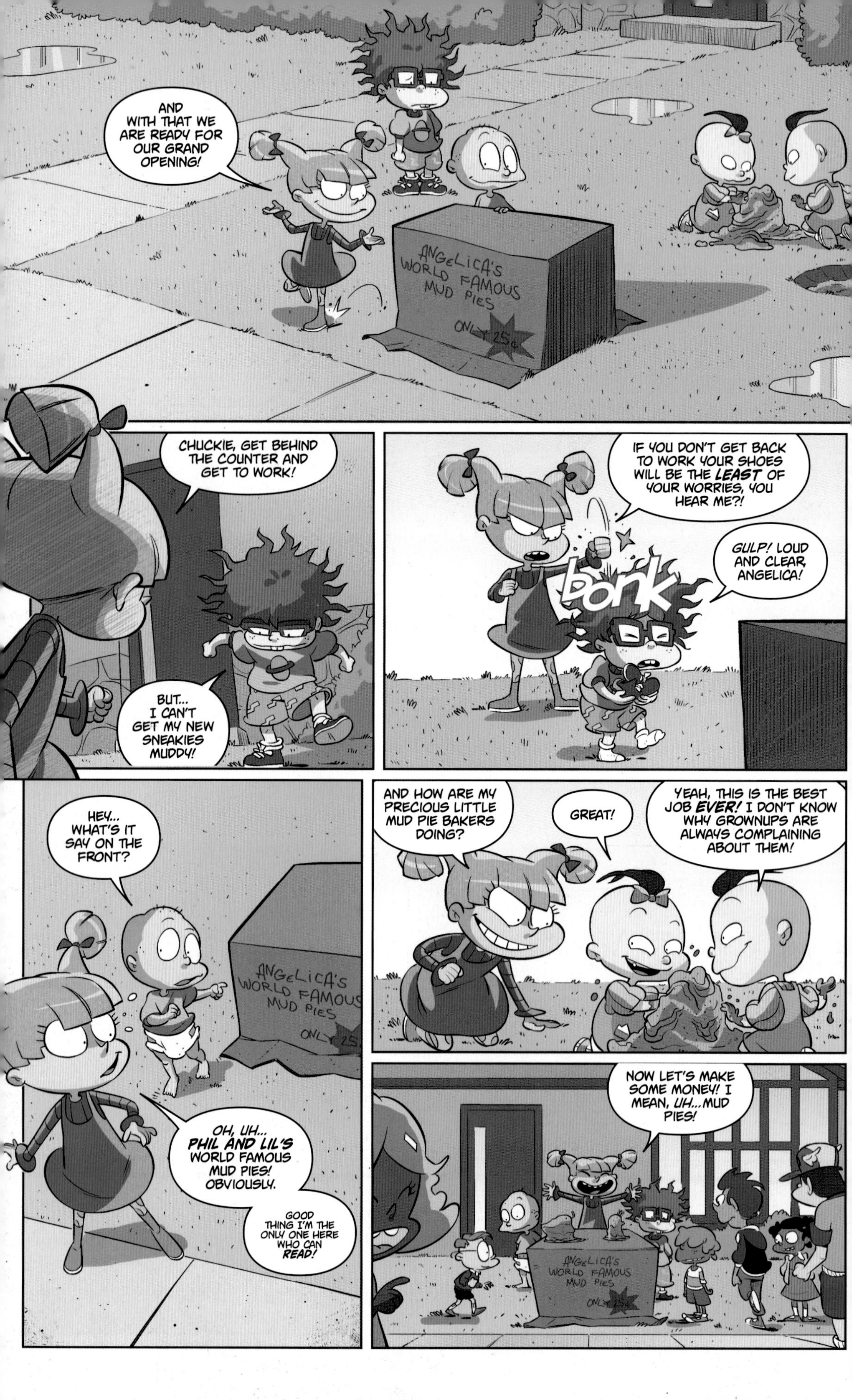
AND WITH THAT WE ARE READY FOR OUR GRAND OPENING!
ANGELICA'S WORLD FAMOUS MUD PIES ONLY 25¢
CHUCKIE, GET BEHIND THE COUNTER AND GET TO WORK!
BUT... I CAN'T GET MY NEW SNEAKIES MUDDY!
IF YOU DON'T GET BACK TO WORK YOUR SHOES WILL BE THE LEAST OF YOUR WORRIES, YOU HEAR ME?!
BONK
GULP! LOUD AND CLEAR, ANGELICA!
HEY... WHAT'S IT SAY ON THE FRONT?
ANGELICA'S WORLD FAMOUS MUD PIES ONLY 25¢
OH, UH... PHIL AND LIL'S WORLD FAMOUS MUD PIES! OBVIOUSLY.
GOOD THING I'M THE ONLY ONE HERE WHO CAN READ!
AND HOW ARE MY PRECIOUS LITTLE MUD PIE BAKERS DOING?
GREAT!
YEAH, THIS IS THE BEST JOB EVER! I DON'T KNOW WHY GROWNUPS ARE ALWAYS COMPLAINING ABOUT THEM!
NOW LET'S MAKE SOME MONEY! I MEAN, UH...MUD PIES!
ANGELICA'S WORLD FAMOUS MUD PIES ONLY 25¢

THANK YOU, COME AGAIN.
THANK YOU, TELL ALL YOUR FRIENDS.
THANK YOU, GIMME YOUR MONEY.
WOW, BUSINESS IS REALLY BOOMING!
YEAH, WHO KNEW KIDS LOVED *MUD* SO MUCH?
ANGELICA'S WORLD FAMOUS MUD PIES
ONLY 25¢
HA HA, AT THIS RATE, I'LL HAVE ENOUGH FOR MY VIDEO GAME BY NAPTIME!
HEY! YOU! COME ON OVER HERE AND BUY SOME MUD PIES!
OH, I'D LOVE TO, BUT WE'RE NOT ALLOWED TO CROSS THE STREET ON OUR OWN!
OUR MOMMY SAYS IT'S TOO DANGEROUS!
GAH! THIS IS TERRIBLE! WE JUST LOST *HALF* OF OUR POTENTIAL CUSTOMERS! IT'S NOT LIKE WE CAN BE IN TWO PLACES AT ONCE!
OR *CAN* WE?

FRENCH FRIES? I MEAN, I GUESS I AM GETTING PRETTY HUNGIE.
GUH, NO, FRANCHISE! DON'T YOU DUMB BABIES KNOW ANYTHING?
ONE OF YOU OPENS UP A SECOND SHOP ACROSS THE STREET AND I GET THE MONEY FROM BOTH.
ONE OF US GOES OVER THERE...BY OURSELVES? NO WAY!
YEAH, ME AND LIL ARE A TEAM!
SPLAT
GAH!
GRRRR, YOU DUMB BABIES!
VERY WELL... WE'LL DO THIS THE HARD WAY.

YOU KNOW, I'VE GOTTEN SOME COMPLAINTS FROM OUR CUSTOMERS...
THEY SAID THEY DON'T LIKE THE WORMS. TOO WIGGLY.
OH, NO PROBLEM! WE'LL JUST CUT THEM OUT!
WHAT?!
YOU CAN'T CUT OUT THE WORMIES! THE WORMIES ARE THE BEST PART!
I DON'T SEE WHAT THE BIG DEAL IS! WORMIES AREN'T EVEN THAT GREAT.
PFFT, YOU WOULD SAY THAT! AFTER ALL, YOU THINK GRASS IS THE BEST PART!
WHA... BUT IT IS!
NUH UH, WORMIES ARE THE BEST!
GRASS IS! IT'S WHAT GIVES IT ITS FLAVOR!
THE WORMS GIVE IT SLIMY TEXTURE! AND IT WIGGLES!
MAYBE... WE SHOULDN'T MAKE MUD PIES TOGETHER ANYMORE.
PHILLIP... WHAT ARE YOU...?
I DON'T NEED YOU, LILLIAN! YOU'RE ALWAYS HOLDING ME BACK! I'M GOING TO GO MAKE MY OWN MUD PIES!
WELL...GOOD! GO! AND TAKE YOUR SMELLY WORMIES WITH YOU!
HA HA HAAAAAAA! ALL THOSE QUARTERS WILL BE MIIIIIIINE!

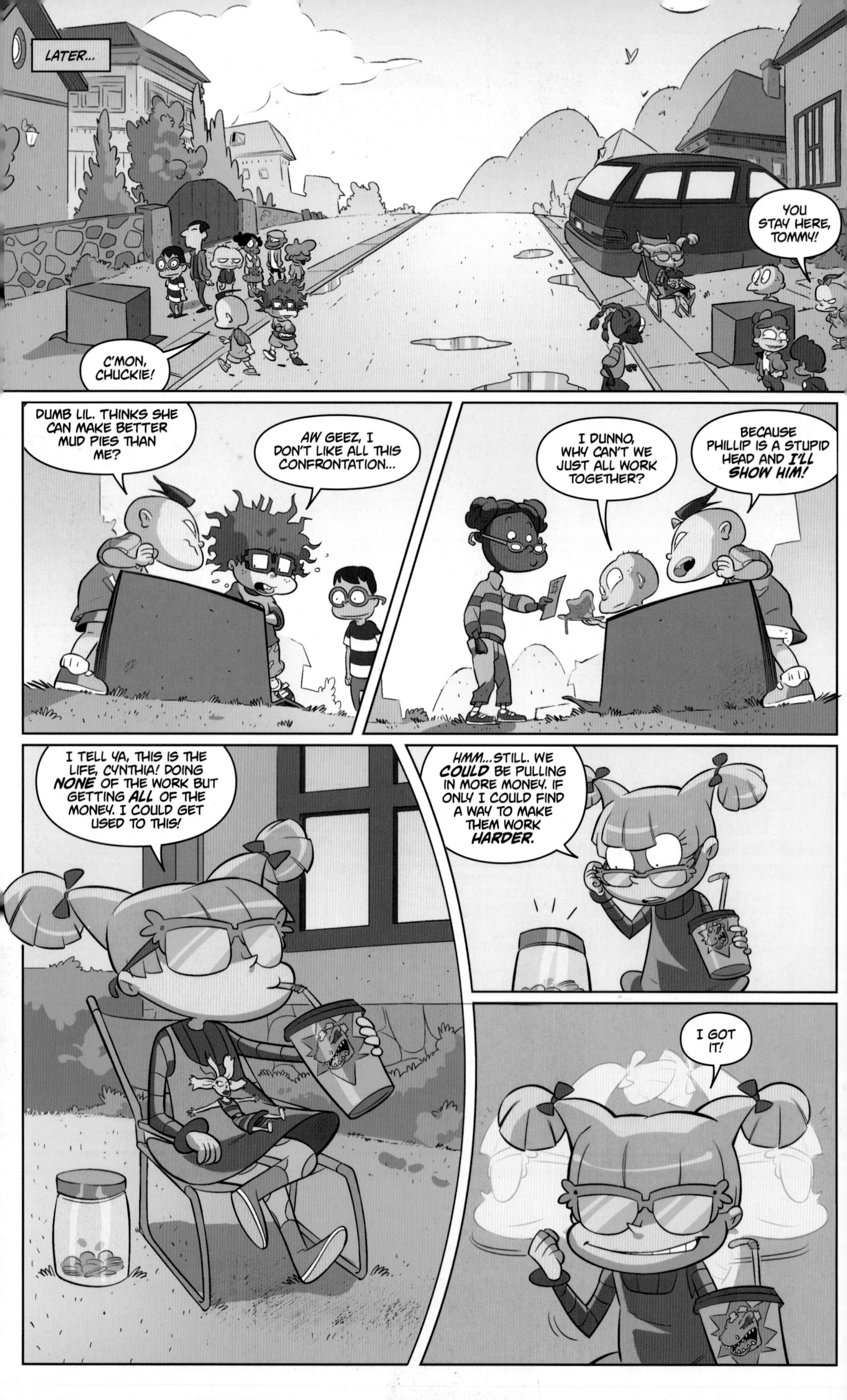
LATER...
C'MON, CHUCKIE!
YOU STAY HERE, TOMMY!
DUMB LIL. THINKS SHE CAN MAKE BETTER MUD PIES THAN ME?
AW GEEZ, I DON'T LIKE ALL THIS CONFRONTATION...
I DUNNO, WHY CAN'T WE JUST ALL WORK TOGETHER?
BECAUSE PHILLIP IS A STUPID HEAD AND I'LL SHOW HIM!
I TELL YA, THIS IS THE LIFE, CYNTHIA! DOING NONE OF THE WORK BUT GETTING ALL OF THE MONEY. I COULD GET USED TO THIS!
HMM...STILL. WE COULD BE PULLING IN MORE MONEY. IF ONLY I COULD FIND A WAY TO MAKE THEM WORK HARDER.
I GOT IT!

SEE, IF I KEEP THEM WRAPPED UP THEY WON'T GET MUDDY!
I JUST THINK BEING CLEAN IS OVERRATED.
HEH HEH HEH!
AAAGGHHHH
MY MUD PIES! WHAT HAPPENED? THEY ARE FILLED WITH PRETTY THINGS!
OH NOOOOO!
I KINDA LIKE THEM!
BUT NO ONE BUYS MUD PIES BECAUSE THEY ARE PRETTY! THEY WANT GOOEY, ICKY, AND GROSS! THIS IS GOING TO TAKE ME FOREVER TO FIX!
YOU KNOW, LIL TOLD ME SHE WAS PLANNING ON SOMETHING LIKE THIS, BUT I NEVER THOUGHT SHE'D STOOP SO LOW! AND TO HER OWN TWIN BROTHER!
LILLIAN!

HERE YA GO, FLUFFY. YOU KNOW WHAT TO DO!
FLUFFY
HEH HEH HEH!
HA HA HAAAAA!
KA-SNAAP
HAHAHA, THIS FIGHTING IS JUST MAKING EVERYONE BUY MORE PIES! I'M GONNA BE A BAZILLIONARE BY DINNER!
HEE HEE, GOOD KITTY!
OH, THIS IS TOO GROSS EVEN FOR ME!
HEY, SOMEONE TIED MY HOSE! I BET IT WAS LIL!
MY SHOVEL! MY BEAUTIFUL SHOVEL!
THAT'S IT!
STOP TRYING TO SAVVY-TAGE* ME!
STOP TRYING TO SAVVY-TAGE ME!
*Editor's Note: savvy-tage = sabotage
BUT I DIDN'T!
YES YOU DID!
NUH UH! YOU DID!
NUH UH! YOU DID!
ANGELICA, WE HAVE TO STOP THIS BEFORE IT GETS OUT OF HAND!
YEAH, BUT SINCE THEY'VE BEEN FIGHTING LIKE THIS PIE SALES HAVE BEEN THROUGH THE ROOF!

THERE'S ONLY ONE WAY TO SETTLE THIS!
YEAH!
MUD FIIIIIIIIIIGHT!
EEK!
ANGELICA, WHAT DO WE DO?!
UHHHHH, I THINK I HEAR MY DAD CALLING ME. BYE!

HMM?
RUMBLE
RUMBLE
MUD FIGHT!
MUD FIGHT!
MUD FIGHT!
MUD FIGHT?
WE'RE HAVING A MUD FIGHT?!
IT IS TIME TO THROW OFF THE SHACKLES OF THE ADULT WORLD AND GIVE IN TO OUR MOST BASIC OF IMPULSES!
TO DIVE BACK INTO OUR PAST AND RECAPTURE THE MAGIC OF THE CAREFREE DAYS OF OUR YOUTH WITH A GOOD OL' FASHIONED MUD FIGHT!
BECAUSE ISN'T THAT WHAT TRULY MAKES LIFE WORTH LIVING? NOT THIS CORPORATE RAT RACE BUT HAPPINESS?
HAROLD!
BUT, I...
HEH...SORRY, HONEY. I'M GOING TO WORK.
SIGH...MY MOTHER WAS RIGHT...

OKAY, YOUR MISSION IS TO TAKE OUT PHILLIP'S STORE AND CUT OFF HIS SUPPLY OF MUD PIES!
GOT IT, BOSS!
WE ARE MAKING OUR WAY TO THE TARGET, OVER!
WHAT? IT'S NOT OVER! IT'S JUST GETTING STARTED!
AND MY NAME IS LIL, NOT ROGER!
ROGER THAT!
WE'VE REACHED THE MUD PIT AND ARE APPROACHING WITH EXTREME CAUTION.
EVERYBODY GET YOUR MUD READY!
AND KEEP YOUR EYES OPEN!

IT'S QUIET.

TOO QUIET.

WE HAVE MOVEMENT!

I GIVE UP, I ***GIVE UP!*** PLEASE, I JUST DON'T WANT MY SNEAKIES GETTING MUDDY!

IT'S OKAY. NOT EVERY BABY IS CUT OUT FOR A MUD WAR. LET'S GET YOU OUT OF HERE.

CAPTAIN, WHAT IS GOING ON OVER THERE?

NICE TRY, LILLIAN.

PHILLIP!

OKAY...THIS IS GETTING TOO INTENSE! I GOTTA GO HIDE WITH MY QUARTERS AND WAIT FOR THIS TO BLOW OVER!
PERFECT!
HEY! BIG KID! HELP ME!
LET ME HIDE WITH YOU!
UHHHHH...
SLAMMO
PLEEEEEEASE! HAVE A HEART!
CLICK
LOOKS LIKE THE END OF THE LINE, SQUIRT!
HUFF... HUFF...
SPLAAAAAT

MY FELLOW BABIES AND KIDS, LISTEN!
WE ARE BETTER THAN THIS! LET'S STOP THIS MADNESS!
LET'S ALL GO BACK TO BEING FRIENDS!
HEH HEH...
TOMMY?
TOMMY, LOOK OUT!
WHA?
GAAHHH!
SPLOORT!
CHUCKIE!
THEY...THEY GOT ME, TOMMY...
JUST HANG IN THERE, IT'S GONNA BE OKAY!
TELL ME... DID...DID THEY GET MY SNEAKIES?
HEY, THEY'RE ALL CLEAN, CHUCKIE!
PHEW! OKAY... I'M JUST GOING TO PASS OUT HERE NOW...

AGGGGGGGHHHHH!

AGGHHHHHHH--

HUH?

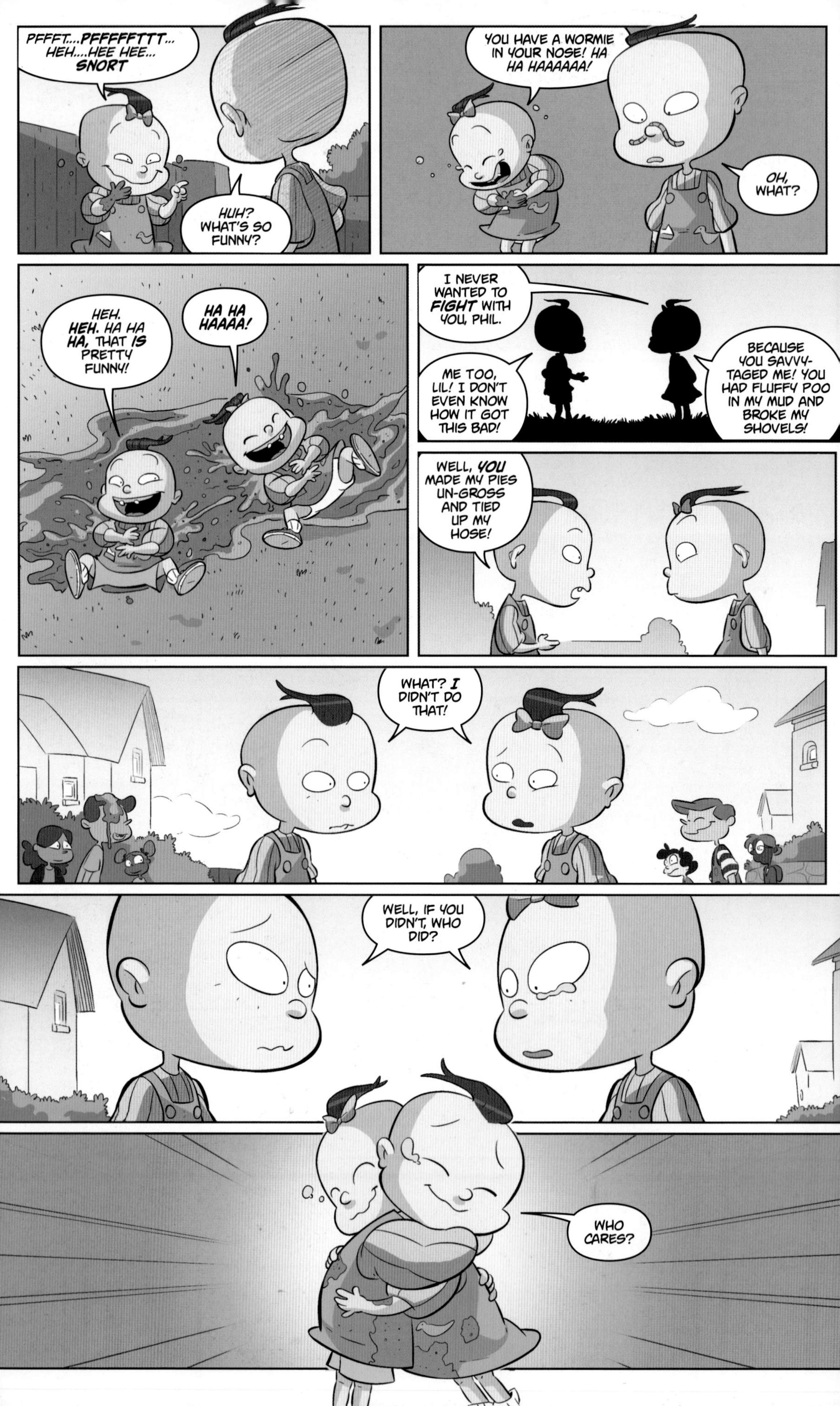
PFFFT....PFFFFFTTT...
HEH....HEE HEE...
SNORT
HUH? WHAT'S SO FUNNY?
YOU HAVE A WORMIE IN YOUR NOSE! HA HA HAAAAAA!
OH, WHAT?
HEH. HEH. HA HA HA, THAT IS PRETTY FUNNY!
HA HA HAAAA!
I NEVER WANTED TO FIGHT WITH YOU, PHIL.
ME TOO, LIL! I DON'T EVEN KNOW HOW IT GOT THIS BAD!
BECAUSE YOU SAVVY-TAGED ME! YOU HAD FLUFFY POO IN MY MUD AND BROKE MY SHOVELS!
WELL, YOU MADE MY PIES UN-GROSS AND TIED UP MY HOSE!
WHAT? I DIDN'T DO THAT!
WELL, IF YOU DIDN'T, WHO DID?
WHO CARES?

SHE DID IT! I SAW IT. I SAW IT ALL! SHE PUT GLITTER IN YOUR PIES, FED HER CAT ROTTEN FISH, TIED YOUR HOSE, AND BROKE YOUR SHOVELS.
EEP.
HEY! YOU DUMB BABIES CAN'T MAKE UP! WE STILL GOT MUD PIES TO SELL!
ANGELICA! HOW COULD YOU?
YEAH, THAT WAS VERY UN-COOL!
BUT...IT'S NOT MY FAULT! I...I JUST WANTED TO BUY A VIDEO GAME! DON'T BLAME ME! BLAME THE SYSTEM!
ANGELICAAAAAAA!
UH OH.
I LEAVE YOU ALONE FOR ELEVEN MINUTES AND THIS IS WHAT HAPPENS? LOOK AT MY LAWN! LOOK AT MY MINIVAN!

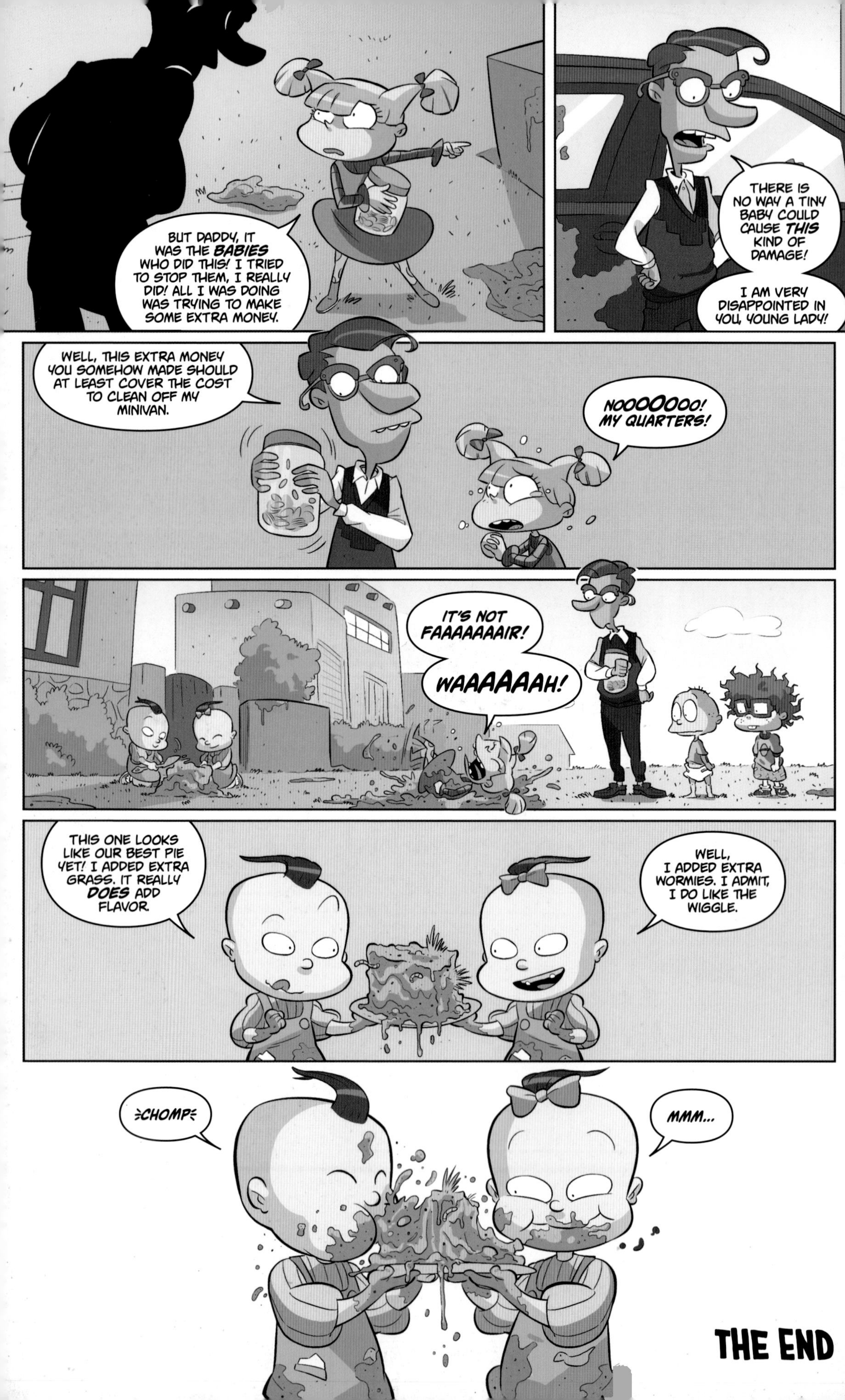
BUT DADDY, IT WAS THE BABIES WHO DID THIS! I TRIED TO STOP THEM, I REALLY DID! ALL I WAS DOING WAS TRYING TO MAKE SOME EXTRA MONEY.
THERE IS NO WAY A TINY BABY COULD CAUSE THIS KIND OF DAMAGE!
I AM VERY DISAPPOINTED IN YOU, YOUNG LADY!
WELL, THIS EXTRA MONEY YOU SOMEHOW MADE SHOULD AT LEAST COVER THE COST TO CLEAN OFF MY MINIVAN.
NOOOOOOO! MY QUARTERS!
IT'S NOT FAAAAAAAIR!
WAAAAAAH!
THIS ONE LOOKS LIKE OUR BEST PIE YET! I ADDED EXTRA GRASS. IT REALLY DOES ADD FLAVOR.
WELL, I ADDED EXTRA WORMIES. I ADMIT, I DO LIKE THE WIGGLE.
CHOMP
MMM...
THE END

YOU CAN'T CUT OUT THE WORMIES! THE WORMIES ARE **THE BEST PART!**

COVER
GALLERY

ISSUE FIVE COVER BY **JORGE CORONA**

ISSUE SIX COVER BY **JORGE CORONA**

ISSUE SEVEN COVER BY **JORGE CORONA**

ISSUE EIGHT COVER BY **JORGE CORONA**

ISSUE FIVE COLORING BOOK COVER BY **JORGE MONLONGO**

ISSUE FIVE EMERALD CITY COMICCON EXCLUSIVE COVER BY **JAY FOSGITT**
WITH COLORS BY **ELEONORA BRUNI**

ISSUE FIVE SUBSCRIPTION COVER BY **DANIEL BAYLISS**
WITH LUNCHBOX DESIGN BY **CAITLYN INGOLDSBY**

ISSUE SIX SUBSCRIPTION COVER BY **DEREK CHARM**
WITH LUNCHBOX DESIGN BY **CAITLYN INGOLDSBY**

ISSUE SEVEN SUBSCRIPTION COVER BY **SARAH SEARLE**
WITH LUNCHBOX DESIGN BY **CAITLYN INGOLDSBY**

ISSUE EIGHT SUBSCRIPTION COVER BY **ELEONORA BRUNI**
WITH LUNCHBOX DESIGN BY **CAITLYN INGOLDSBY**